Writing Stories
Mystery Stories

Anita Ganeri

Raintree is an imprint of Capstone Global Library Limited, a company incorporated in England and Wales having its registered office at 7 Pilgrim Street, London, EC4V 6LB – Registered company number: 6695582

www.raintreepublishers.co.uk
myorders@raintreepublishers.co.uk

Edited by Dan Nunn, Rebecca Rissman, and Sian Smith
Designed by Joanna Hinton-Malivoire
Original illustrations © Capstone Global Library 2013
Picture research by Ruth Blair
Production by Sophia Argyris
Originated by Capstone Global Library Ltd
Printed and bound in China

ISBN 978 1 406 26038 0 (hardback)
17 16 15 14 13
10 9 8 7 6 5 4 3 2 1

ISBN 978 1 406 26045 8 (paperback)
17 16 15 14 13
10 9 8 7 6 5 4 3 2 1

British Library Cataloguing in Publication Data
Ganeri, Anita, 1961-
Mystery stories. -- (Writing stories) 1. Detective and mystery stories--Authorship--Juvenile literature. 2. Detective and mystery stories. 3. Children's stories.
I. Title II. Series
808.3'872-dc23

Acknowledgements
We would like to thank the following for permission to reproduce photographs: Shutterstock, background images and design, pp.4 (© Kamira), 5 (© Zurijeta), 6 (© Fer Gregory), 7 (© Richard Peterson), 8 & 9 (© Monkey Business Images), 12 (© Chad Zuber), 14 (© alsamua), 16 (© Neda Sadreddin), 16 & 22 (© HiSunnySky), 24 (© A.Krotov), 24 (© zhykova), 26 (© Nattika).

Cover photographs reproduced with permission of istockphoto (© GaryAlvis) and Shutterstock (© VikaSuh, © Hywit Dimyadi).

Every effort has been made to contact copyright holders of material reproduced in this book. Any omissions will be rectified in subsequent printings if notice is given to the publisher.

All the Internet addresses (URLs) given in this book were valid at the time of going to press. However, due to the dynamic nature of the Internet, some addresses may have changed, or sites may have changed or ceased to exist since publication. While the author and publisher regret any inconvenience this may cause readers, no responsibility for any such changes can be accepted by either the author or the publisher.

Some words are shown in bold, like this. You can find out what they mean by looking in the glossary.

Contents

Follow this symbol to read a mystery story.

What is a story?

A story is a piece of **fiction** writing. It describes made-up people, places, and events. Before you start writing your story, you need to work out a **setting**, **characters**, and a **plot**.

There are lots of different types of stories. You can write spooky stories, silly stories, fairy tales, adventure stories, animal stories, and lots more. This book is about writing mystery stories.

Mystery stories

A mystery story needs an exciting mystery to solve, someone to **investigate** the mystery, clues, and **suspects**. When you start writing, you should know how the mystery is solved but make sure you do not give it away too soon.

Sherlock Holmes is a detective who stars in a series of mystery stories, written by Arthur Conan Doyle. The stories are set in London about 100 years ago. Holmes is famous for solving mysteries that no one else can solve.

Story ideas

Get some ideas for your story before you start writing. Look in books, on the internet or TV, or use your imagination. You should also read lots of mystery stories by other writers. This can help to spark off ideas.

Jot down your ideas in a notebook so
that you do not forget them. Then you
can look at them when you start writing.
Always keep your notebook handy, even
at night. You never know when a brilliant
idea will come.

What happens next?

What happens in your mystery story? This is called the **plot**. The plot needs a beginning, a middle, and an end. You can try using a **story mountain**, like the one below, to help you work out your plot.

Middle
The main action happens. There may be a problem for one of your characters.

Beginning
Set the scene and introduce your main **characters**.

Ending
The problem is solved and the story ends.

Your story starts at one side of the mountain, goes up to the top, then down the other side.

When you are planning your plot, you need to put events in the right order. You can use a **timeline** to help you. Here is a timeline for the mystery story in this book.

Mum finds the biscuit tin empty.
⬇
She searches the kitchen.
⬇
Mum asks Dad and Harry if they ate the biscuits.
⬇
Harry sets about solving the mystery.
⬇
Harry looks for clues.
⬇
Harry interviews the main **suspects.**
⬇
Harry lays a trap to catch the thief.
⬇
The biscuit thief is caught.

In the beginning

The beginning of your story is where something happens to get your story started. It should grab your readers' attention and make them want to keep reading. It is also where you introduce your main **characters**.

"That's strange," thought Mum, peering into the biscuit tin. "It's empty."

The start of your story should draw your readers in.

A Mystery Story

"That's strange," thought Mum, peering into the biscuit tin. "It's empty."

She turned it upside down, just to make sure.

"I'm sure that I filled it up yesterday," she thought. "Dad and Harry can't have eaten them all!"

 Can you think of another way of starting this story?

Crime scene

The **setting** is the place and time in which your story happens. You can set a mystery story somewhere dramatic, such as in a deep, dark wood, or in an old, creaky hotel. You can also set it somewhere ordinary, such as at school or at home.

In a mystery story, the setting may also be a **crime scene**.

Mum looked around the kitchen. Everything else seemed to be in the right place. She looked in all the cupboards. She searched on all the shelves. She looked in the fridge. She looked in the dog's bowl. But she couldn't find the missing biscuits anywhere.

Add more details to the description to bring your setting to life.

Character files

Creating strong **characters** is very important. You want your readers to care about them and believe in them. Write fact files for your main characters. Think about what the characters look like and how they think, feel, and behave.

Character fact file
Character: Mum
Age: not saying
Looks like: short; glasses; long, brown hair
Personality: kind; a bit forgetful
Likes: having a biscuit with her cup of tea
Dislikes: when the biscuits go missing

Character fact file
Character: Harry
Age: 8
Looks like: medium height; short, brown hair
Personality: helpful; clever; curious
Likes: dogs; detective stories
Dislikes: getting blamed for everything

Mum and Harry are two of the main characters in our story.

When Harry got back from school, Mum was waiting with the empty tin.

"Anything to tell me, Harry?" she asked as she pointed to the tin.

"Maybe you left them somewhere Mum," said Harry. "I mean, you do, er, lose things sometimes."

Mum tried again when Dad got home.

"They're probably in the dog," said Dad. "He always looks hungry."

 Ordinary people can make interesting characters, too.

In the middle

The middle of your story is where the main action happens. This is where your **characters** face a tricky problem or have a mystery to solve. You might have several ideas about what happens next. Here are two possible **plots** for our story.

The biscuits have gone missing.

1. Harry tries to solve the mystery.

2. Mum finds the biscuits. The dog has buried them in his bed.

Can you think of any other plot ideas?

Suddenly, Harry rushed up to his room. When he came back, he was clutching a magnifying glass and a large notebook.

"Don't worry, Mum," he said. "Detective Harry — and his dog — are here to solve the Mystery of the Missing Biscuits."

"Humph," said Dad. "I expect that means you'll want a reward."

Mind mapping

Even the best writers sometimes get stuck about what to write. If you need help to work out what happens next, try using a **mind map**. Write down a key word or idea. Then jot down other words or ideas that are connected to it.

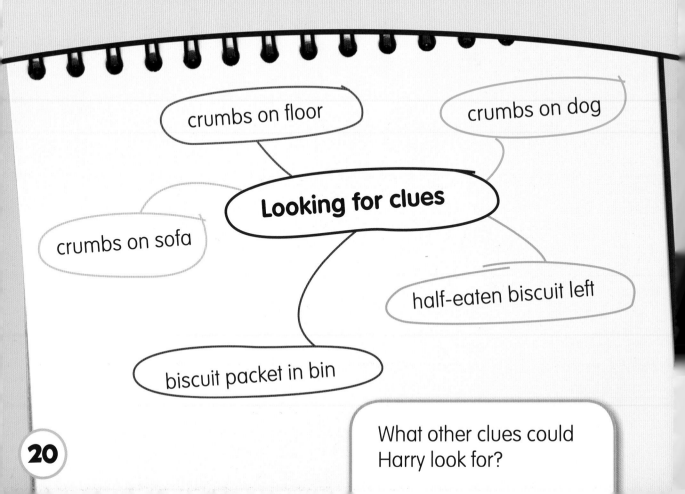

crumbs on floor

crumbs on dog

Looking for clues

crumbs on sofa

half-eaten biscuit left

biscuit packet in bin

What other clues could Harry look for?

Harry began searching for clues. He didn't have to look very hard. He found biscuit crumbs on the hall carpet and on the kitchen floor. There were even biscuit crumbs on the dog.

"I wonder what that's doing there?" said Harry, picking up a half-eaten biscuit from Dad's bedside table.

You need to keep the story moving on, without giving the answer to the mystery away.

Speaking parts

Dialogue means the words people say. Adding dialogue to your story helps to bring it to life and to make your **characters** more believable. Try to think about how each of your characters might sound if they spoke out loud.

"Mum," he said. "How many biscuits have you had today?"

Put **speech marks** around the spoken words.

Next, Harry decided to interview the chief suspects.

"Mum," he said. "How many biscuits have you had today?"

"Er, none," said Mum. "That's the problem."

"Dad," said Harry. "Can you explain what this biscuit was doing in your bedroom?"

"Haven't a clue," said Dad. "It'll be that dog. Ask him."

Dialogue can help your readers to learn more about your characters.

Mystery writing

In a mystery story, it is important to make your writing exciting. Choose your words carefully. For example, you can use lots of different **adjectives**, **adverbs**, and **verbs** to add interesting details to your writing.

That night, after Mum and Dad had gone to bed, Harry <u>sneaked</u> downstairs and set up a <u>cunning</u> trap for the biscuit thief.

Sneaked is a verb. *Cunning* is an adjective.

That night, after Mum and Dad had gone to bed, Harry sneaked downstairs and set up a cunning trap for the biscuit thief. He put new biscuits in the tin and left it on the kitchen table. Then he tied a long piece of string around the tin. He tied the other end around his finger. Finally, Harry went into the lounge next door, settled down on the sofa, and fell fast asleep.

 Use sentences of different lengths to add interest.

Whodunnit?

The ending of your story is where you solve the mystery and tie up any loose ends. Try not to give the ending away earlier in the story. Then it will come as a surprise to your readers.

Possible endings

Mum had left the biscuits in the bathroom.

Dad had been eating the biscuits in his sleep.

The dog had buried the biscuits in the garden.

Can you think of any more endings?

A few hours later, Harry felt a tug on his finger. He crept into the kitchen. A shadowy figure was munching a biscuit. The biscuit thief was... Dad!

"Got you, Dad!" said Harry, but Dad didn't seem to hear him. He was still fast asleep!

"I had a funny dream last night," said Dad, next morning. Mum and Harry said nothing. They just looked at each other and grinned.

Use your ending to tell your readers what happens to your **characters**.

27

More top tips

1 Read some mystery stories by other writers. This will help you to improve your own writing and may spark off ideas.

2 Don't give away your mystery too soon. It will spoil the ending if the reader knows "whodunnit" too early in the story.

3 Keep your readers guessing by having several **suspects**. You can also add some false clues.

4 Always read your story through when you have finished. Spot and correct any mistakes. You may need to do this several times.

5 A mystery story should be exciting. Use short sentences to speed up the **pace** of your writing and add excitement.

6 Think of a great title for your story. Choose something that will make people keen to read the story.

Glossary

adjectives describing words that tell you about a noun (a noun is a naming word)

adverbs describing words that tell you about a verb (a verb is a doing word)

characters people in a piece of writing

crime scene place where a crime happens

dialogue words that characters say

fiction writing about made-up things

investigate find out about a mystery or crime

mind map diagram of ideas on a subject

pace speed at which a story moves along

plot what happens in a story

setting time and place in which a story is set

speech marks marks that show spoken words

story mountain diagram for planning a story

suspect person who could have carried out a crime

timeline list of events and when they happen

verbs doing or action words

Find out more

Books

How to Write Stories, Celia Warren (QED Publishing, 2008)

Writing Stories, Anita Ganeri (Raintree Publishing, 2013)

Write Your Own Story Book, Louie Stowell and Jane Chisholm (Usborne Publishing, 2011)

Websites

www.bbc.co.uk/schools/ks2bitesize/english/writing
Learn how to improve your writing skills on this website.

www.readwritethink.org/files/resources/interactives/cube_creator/
The writing cubes on this website will help you to create your own stories.

31

Index